Jesse Bear, What Will You Wear?

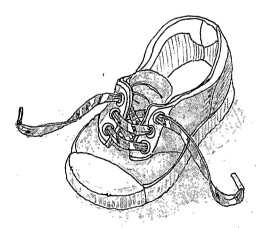

Jesse Bear,
What Will You Wear?

by Nancy White Carlstrom
illustrations by Bruce Degen

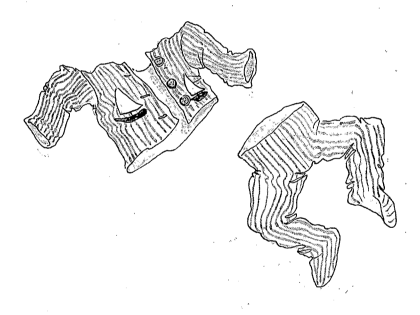

Macmillan Publishing Company
New York

Collier Macmillan Publishers
London

Macmillan Publishing Company
866 Third Avenue, New York, N.Y. 10022
Collier Macmillan Canada, Inc.

Printed and bound by South China Printing Company, Hong Kong
First American Edition

10   9   8   7   6   5   4   3   2   1

The text of this book is set in 18 pt. Goudy Old Style.
The illustrations are rendered in pen-and-ink
and watercolor and reproduced in full color.

Library of Congress Cataloging in Publication Data

Carlstrom, Nancy White.
Jesse Bear, what will you wear?

Summary: Rhymed text and illustrations describe
Jesse Bear's activities from morning to bedtime.
[1. Bears—Fiction. 2. Stories in rhyme]
I. Degen, Bruce, ill. II. Title.
PZ8.3.C1948Je   1986   [E]   85-10610
ISBN 0-02-717350-X

To Jesse David,
the real Jesse Bear,
with love
— N.W.C.

For Denny, Lisa, and Brian
— B.D.

Jesse Bear, what will you wear?
What will you wear in the morning?

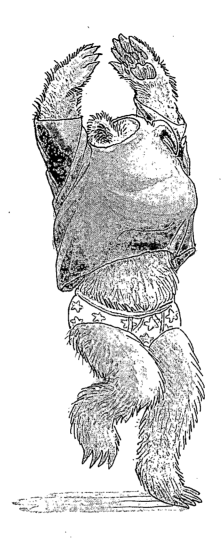

My shirt of red
Pulled over my head
Over my head in the morning.

I'll wear my pants
My pants that dance
My pants that dance in the morning.

I'll wear a rose
Between my toes
A rose in my toes in the morning.

I'll wear the sun
On my legs that run
Sun on the run in the morning.

I'll wear the sand
On my arm and hand
Sand on my hand in the morning.

Jesse Bear, what will you wear
What will you wear at noon?

I'll wear my chair.
You'll wear your chair?

I'll wear my chair
'Cause I'm stuck there
Stuck in my chair at noon.

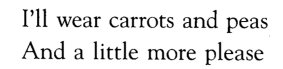

I'll wear carrots and peas
And a little more please

Celery crunch
And sprouts in a bunch

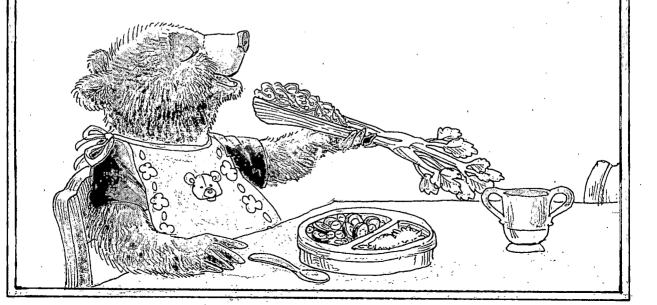

An apple to bite
And a moustache of white

Juice from a pear
And rice in my hair
That's what I'll wear at noon.

Jesse Bear, what will you wear
What will you wear at night?

Not my shirt
It's covered with dirt
Not my pants
That sat in the ants
Ants in my pants tonight.

Jesse Bare, what will you wear
What will you wear at night?
Water to float
My bubbles and boat
I'll wear in the tub tonight.

My pj's with feet
And face on the seat

My blanket that's blue
And plays peek-a-boo

Bear hugs from you
And three kisses too
That's what I'll wear tonight.

Jesse Bear, what will you wear
What will you wear at night?

Sleep in my eyes
And stars in the skies
Moon on my bed
And dreams in my head
That's what I'll wear tonight.